MW00974798

The privilege of a lifetime is to become who you truly are.

—C.G. Jung

How many times does Buddy Bee appear in this book?
Don't forget to count the cover, too!
(Answer is on copyright page.)

Compare Bear's DOUBLE DARE

KIM LINETTE

illustrated by James Loram

KAPALUA COVE

“GRRR, get lost kid!” growled Bear from behind the bushes.

GRRR

“YIKES, Mr. Bear. I can’t ‘get lost.’ I’m ALREADY lost,” said Danny with a chuckle as he tried to see the bear through the branches. “Mr. Bear, I’d be happy to go away if you’d just show me the way back. I went for a hike this morning and lost the trail.”

“GRRR, don’t come any closer, kid, or I’ll swipe you with my big paw!” said Bear.

“Mr. Bear, why would a big bear like you want to hide from a kid like me? Besides, I’ve never seen a bear in the wild before. Will you please come out from behind those bushes?”

“No,” grumbled Bear. “And STOP calling me ‘Mr. Bear.’ I have a name, you know.”

“Of course,” said Danny. “Let me introduce myself. My name is Danny. Some people call me ‘Daring Danny.’ You want to know why? It’s because I LOVE to do new things, especially when they take some courage. That’s why I decided to go hiking this morning. I’ve never been on a hike before. I wasn’t sure if I’d be any good at it. So, I decided to give it a try, and here I am!

“Now it’s your turn, Mr. Bear. What’s YOUR name?”

“Well if you MUST know, my name is Compare. Compare Bear,” said the bear.

“Compare Bear? That’s a very unusual name. How did you get it?”

“Hmmf! I don’t like my name, and I don’t want to talk about it,” grumbled Compare Bear.

“Okay,” said Danny. “You don’t have to tell me. But at least come out from those bushes. I feel kind of silly standing here talking to a bush.”

“Nice to meet you, Compare Bear,” said Danny. “I’ve never met a bear before!”

“Hey, I have an idea! See those trees over there? Let’s go climb them! I hear bears are great at climbing, and maybe from up top we can spot my trail.”

“NO—not me!” stated Compare firmly. “I don’t climb trees. I used to, but not anymore.”

“A bear that doesn’t like to climb trees?” asked Danny. “Why not?”

“Well, if you must know,” said Compare Bear, “one day I saw a squirrel racing up a tree. She climbed much faster and higher than I ever could. When I saw I couldn’t climb as well as a squirrel, I decided I would never climb a tree again.”

"Compare Bear! Look at your tail!" shouted Danny.

"Oh no," said Compare, as he tried to hide his new tail. "Why did I ever come out from behind those bushes?"

"Hmmm, that IS one unusual tail for a bear!" said Danny. "But hey, tell me this, Compare Bear. Why would seeing a squirrel make you stop doing something YOU love?"

POOF!

"I decided there was no point," said Compare. "I would never be better than, or even as good as, the squirrels, so why even try anymore?"

"I understand," said Danny. "I remember when I was learning to draw, and my friend drew much better than I did. I wanted to quit too. But then my teacher said, 'Danny, the only person you need to be better than is who you were yesterday!' And you know what? She was right! I've been drawing ever since. And I've gotten pretty good, if I say so myself!"

"Okay, Compare Bear," said Danny. "I have another idea. Let's have a race instead! I hear that bears can run really fast. I know you'll beat me, but I'd LOVE to be able to say I raced a bear!" said Danny.

"No way!" said Compare. "I wouldn't dare. In fact, I haven't gone running for the past year."

"Why not?" asked Danny.

"I'll tell you," said Compare Bear. "Have you ever seen a coyote run? I have, and they are FAST. I used to think I ran fast until I saw a coyote race through the forest. That's when I realized I couldn't run very fast compared to a coyote. So, I stopped running."

POOF!

"Uh-oh," said Danny. "I think I'm beginning to understand why your name is Compare Bear. Every time you compare yourself to someone else and then decide to stop being yourself, a part of YOU changes!

"And, as interesting as those new legs LOOK, I do prefer your original legs," chuckled Danny.

"Compare Bear," said Danny putting his arm around the bear, "why would you want to be like someone else anyway?

"What if the moon compared itself to the sun? Both shine in their own ways and at just the right time. What if the moon stopped shining, just because it's not as bright as the sun?"

“Hmm,” said Compare Bear, with a bit of a smile.

“Now those coyote legs?” laughed Danny. “They are going to be a challenge! I guess running is out. Hmm, what else can we do for fun?

“I know! Compare, come over here! See this cave? How about if you roar into it as loud as you can? I bet you can shake the whole cave with your voice!"

“Nope,” said Compare Bear. “I wouldn’t dare. I used to love to growl and roar, but one day I heard a bird—”

“STOP,” said Danny. “Don’t say it!”

POOF!

"Yep," squeaked Compare Bear, apologetically. "The bird's voice was so much prettier than mine. I was ashamed of my loud roars. So now, I don't roar anymore."

"Oh boy," said Danny, trying to hold back a giggle. "I wish I could have heard you roar. You know, your voice is so deep and growly, your roar would have sounded awesome!"

“Okay,” said Danny, as he hurried over to the pond. “I have another idea. What we need is a purpose. We can’t get distracted by comparing if we just stay focused on a purpose!

“All this hiking has made me hungry,” continued Danny. “Finding lunch would be a great purpose. Let’s go fishing. I KNOW bears are great at fishing . . .

“No!” cried Danny as he looked at Compare’s face. “Compare, you HAVE to like fishing!”

“Well,” squeaked Compare Bear. “I used to like fishing. Until one day I noticed how good the ducks were at fishing. They just float along and pop their heads into the water, and . . . done! Fish caught. That’s when I decided never to get in the water again.”

Danny stared at Compare Bear. Then, looking in the pond, he started to laugh, "Compare Bear, come here. There's something I DO want you to compare!"

POOF!

“Now Compare,” asked Danny, “who would you rather be: bits and pieces of all these other animals . . . ”

"... or your original self?"

Compare Bear started to laugh a squeaky laugh, "Tee, Hee, Hee."

Then, he broke out into a roaring, loud, bear-sized laugh, "ROAR! Ha Ha! ROAR!"

POOF!

"Compare Bear," cheered Danny. "You have your snout back!

"I've got another idea! Today I am going to give you a DOUBLE DARE.

"First: from now on, when you're afraid to do something just because you might not be as good as others, I dare you to . . . DO IT ANYWAY!

"And second: from now on, I dare you to . . . BE 100% YOURSELF!

"After all, you are the only YOU in the entire world. And no one can ever be you . . . better than YOU!"

“Will you do that, Compare Bear? Will you take my double dare?” asked Danny.

“Why . . . yes! Yes, I will!” said Compare in his loudest bear-voice.

“You know what, Danny?” said Compare Bear, with more confidence than before. “All this daring is making me really hungry. How about we go catch some fish?”

POOF!

"Hey Danny, I dare YOU to race me to those trees over there!" yelled Compare Bear as he took off running.

“That was awesome, Compare Bear! Now I can say I raced a bear. I lost by a lot,” laughed Danny, “but I DID race a bear!

“You know, Compare, there is only one thing left to do now,” said Danny, pointing to the tops of the trees.

“I’ll see you at the top!” said Compare Bear as he started climbing.

"Nice work, Compare Bear! We found my trail, and look at your tail! You are back to your original, wonderful self. Thank you for a really great day!" said Danny. "And speaking of today, do you know what I'm going to do TODAY?"

“No, I don’t,” said Compare Bear.

“Today I’m giving you a NEW name,” said Danny. “From now on, I’m going to call you . . . ”

"DARE BEAR!"
DARE
BEAR
COMPARE
BEAR

LET'S EXPLORE!

Share a time when you compared yourself to someone else.

- How did you feel about yourself?
- Did it change the way you acted?
- The next time you are tempted to compare yourself to others, what could you do instead?

Share a time when you were brave and dared to be yourself.

- How did you feel about yourself?
- What are some things that are unique about you?

FUN FACTS ABOUT BEARS

1. A baby bear is called a cub. A female bear is called a sow or she-bear. A male bear is called a boar or a he-bear. A group of bears is called a sleuth or sloth.
2. There are eight species of bear: Asiatic black bear, black bear, brown bear, panda bear, polar bear, sloth bear, spectacled bear, and sun bear. Compare Bear is a brown (grizzly) bear.
3. Bears can run as fast as 40 mph (64 kmph), faster than any human. They are also good swimmers; some can swim over 30 miles (48 kilometers) at a time.
4. Bears have excellent senses of smell, sight, and hearing. They can sense food, other bears, or predators miles away.
5. Bears communicate using about seven or eight different "words" or vocalizations such as: huffs, chomps, groans, roars, woofs, growls, hums, and/or barks.

For the children of this remarkable planet and for those who nurture and care for them.

Forever thanks to my husband, Steve, and to our six children: Michael, Nicholas, Chad, Riley, Brooke, and Dylan, for exploring with me and inspiring me as I've watched you create your own big, happy lives!

Special acknowledgment to Alli, James, and Elynn, whose exceptional talent and professionalism helped bring this adventure to life.

—K.L.

Buddy Bee appears 16 times in this book, including the cover.

100% of profits from EQ Explorers books help nurture and empower underserved children. Kapalua Cove provides direct donations to charitable initiatives and donates books to orphanages, remote libraries, care centers, and more.

For additional reading and resources visit: EQExplorers.com

For information, please contact: info@kapaluacove.com

Cover and Illustrations by James Loram, represented by Lemonade Illustration Agency

ISBN 978-1-950062-01-0

Library of Congress Control Number: 2019938715

Printed in Malaysia

First Edition

1 3 5 7 9 10 8 6 4 2

End notes from front flap:

1. http://adultdevelopment.wix.com/harvardstudy; Travis Bradberry and Jean Greaves, *Emotional Intelligence 2.0*, (San Diego: Talent Smart, 2009)
2. Dr. John Gottman, Raising an Emotionally Intelligent Child (New York: Fireside Books, 1998)